my
little
Treasury

Bedtime Stories

pi kids®
publications international, ltd.

Contents

Puss in Boots

Adapted from the English fairy tale
Illustrated by Jacqueline East

Once upon a time, there lived a clever cat named Puss. One day, Puss lost his owner, a poor farmer. Puss was alone, with nobody to take care of or to take care of him.

Puss decided to find a new owner, and chose the farmer's son. Puss approached the young man and politely said, "Please take me home with you."

"I can't help you," said the young man.

"I am no trouble," said Puss. "I'll even help you. Just give me boots and an old sack."

"All right," laughed the young man.

Puss followed the young man home, where they found a pair of boots and a sack.

"I don't understand what you want with boots and an old sack," the young man said.

Puss smiled, put the boots on, picked up the sack, and headed into the forest.

As he walked, Puss gathered grass. He filled the sack with the green grass he picked. Finding a tree, Puss dropped the sack, closed his eyes, and pretended to be asleep.

Soon, a rabbit hopped by, smelling the fresh grass. The rabbit crawled inside the sack and — *THWAP!* — Puss snatched it right up!

With the rabbit in the sack and the sack on his back, Puss headed to the king's castle.

Arriving at the castle, Puss was ushered into the great throne room.

"Your Highness," the cat said, "I have brought you a gift from my master, the Duke of Cataclaws."

"What is it?" the king asked, and Puss presented him with the splendid rabbit.

The king was glad that the Duke of Cataclaws would send such a fine gift. Little did the king know that there was no Duke of Cataclaws, or that he'd been tricked by a cat.

The rest of the week, Puss gave the king gifts. He brought tasty trout, fat pheasants, and plump partridges. As Puss gave each gift, he said it was from the Duke of Cataclaws.

One day the king decided to take a ride through his kingdom. He took with him his beautiful daughter, the princess.

Puss hurried back home to his master. He told the young man, "You must take off your clothes and jump into the pond by the road."

As the young man hopped in the pond, the royal carriage came down the road. Puss ran to meet it, crying, "Help! The Duke of Cataclaws has been tossed into the water!"

"The Duke of Cataclaws?" asked the king. "Guards, help this man, lest he drown!"

As the king's guards rushed to the young man's aid, Puss sneaked up to the king's carriage and poked his head inside.

"Hello," Puss greeted the princess.

"I am worried about the Duke of Cataclaws," she said. "What happened?"

"He was robbed by hoodlums," Puss said. "The robbers took all of his money. But the king's guards have saved him."

The guards brought the wet young man to the carriage. "Find the duke a dry set of clothes," the king ordered.

"Father, can the duke ride in the carriage with us?" the princess asked the king.

Before the young man knew what was going on, Puss answered, "The duke accepts."

With that, the cat ran ahead of the king's carriage, for he had more work to do.

After running and running, Puss came to some farmers.

"Hello, my fine fellows," said the cat. "You look like you are working hard."

"We work these fields for the giant who lives in yonder castle," said a farmer.

"If we don't work hard, he'll gobble us up," said another farmer.

"About that giant," said Puss, "the king has just named him the Duke of Cataclaws. Now, the king's carriage will come by soon. Make sure you tell the king that the castle belongs to the Duke of Cataclaws."

Next, Puss ran to the castle. For his plan to work, he still had to deal with the giant.

At the castle, Puss found a terrible giant.

"I have heard many great things about you," Puss said. "I have heard that you can turn yourself into any animal that you wish."

"It's true," said the giant. "I can turn into a lion, a bear, or even a great whale."

"But I doubt you could turn into a tiny animal, like a mouse," Puss said.

To prove Puss wrong, the giant turned himself into a mouse—which the cat gobbled right up.

Soon the carriage arrived. Puss said, "Welcome to the castle of the Duke of Cataclaws!" The young man smiled at his cat and his new home.

Rocking-Horse Land

Adapted from the fairy tale by Laurence Housman
Illustrated by Bandelin-Dacey Studios

There once lived a prince named Little Prince Freedling. One morning, Little Prince Freedling rose out of bed like a rocket, as it was a special day.

It was his fifth birthday, and all of the church bells and grandfather clocks in the kingdom announced it at this early hour.

But the prince did not make it past the foot of his bed, for there he found piles of beautifully wrapped birthday gifts.

The first gift that Freedling unwrapped was from his fairy godmother. The note attached to the gift read: "Break me and I shall turn into something else." And the toy did just that. What started out as a top changed once Freedling broke it. In just one hour, the toy became a jump rope, a ship, building blocks, a jigsaw puzzle, a drum, a kaleidoscope, a whistle, and a thousand other things. It became a kite, and its string broke. Off it flew, never to be seen again.

Little Prince Freedling looked for another gift. He found one by his window: a great, golden rocking horse.

Freedling ran to the window and threw his arms around the horse's neck. The horse's big eyes shone so bright, they almost seemed alive. The prince climbed on the horse's back and spent the day there, chasing dragons and villains in his bedroom.

That night, Freedling woke up longing to see his rocking horse once more. The prince was shocked to find that the horse was not where he had left it. Instead, it had crossed his bedroom and stood staring out the window into the dark, dark night.

Freedling saw that its eyes were full of tears that shone in the starlight.

"Why are you crying?" Freedling asked.

To Freedling's surprise, the rocking horse answered, "Because I am not free. Won't you let me go?" it asked.

"Will you come back?" asked Freedling.

The horse said, "My name is Rollonde. My brothers call me to Rocking-Horse Land. Look in my mane and find the one black hair. Pluck it and wrap it around your finger. As long as you have that hair, you are my master, and I shall return to you each morning."

The prince threw open the window and called, "Rollonde, go to Rocking-Horse Land, but please return to me come morning!"

Rollonde spent the night in the sky. In the morning, he returned to the prince.

A year passed, with Freedling riding Rollonde each day and setting him free each night. Soon the prince awoke to his sixth birthday. The bells and clocks called to him. The gifts sat wrapped at the foot of his bed. The first that Freedling opened was from his fairy godmother. This gift turned out to be a parrot. When the prince pulled the bird's tail, it became a striped lizard. When the prince pulled the lizard's tail, it became a border collie. But when he pulled the pup's tail, it became a Manx cat, which has no tail. Seeing this, the prince looked for his next gift.

The king presented the prince with the finest young stallion in the kingdom.

Prince Freedling spent that day riding his new horse. In fact, he completely forgot about his rocking horse, Rollonde.

That night, as Freedling fell alseep, he heard a crying from beside his bed. The prince looked up to find Rollonde standing there, tears streaming down his face.

"You have a real horse of your own. May I go to Rocking-Horse Land for good?" wept Rollonde.

Freedling threw open the shutters and let Rollonde gallop off into the night sky.

The prince watched the horse go to Rocking-Horse Land. Then he took the black hair from his finger and let it float away, too.

When Little Prince Freedling
had grown up to become King
Freedling, it was the fifth birthday
of his own son, the new prince.
Beautifully wrapped gifts filled the
prince's bedroom, including a
beautiful, golden rocking-horse colt.
The king knelt down and saw
that the colt looked so much like
his own beloved rocking horse.
He searched its mane until he found a
black hair. Plucking the hair, the king gently
wrapped it around the prince's finger, sure
that the prince would take good care of the
son of his old friend, Rollonde.

The Boy Who Cried Wolf

Adapted from the fable by Aesop
Illustrated by Jon Goodell

Once there was a little village called Schaffenburg. Schaffenburg was much like any other little village, except for one thing—its many sheep. The village had so many sheep that the woolly creatures outnumbered the people!

These sheep were famous for what they provided—wool. They had the finest wool in the land. People came from far and wide to get things made from Schaffenburg wool.

Because they depended on the sheep's wool, the villagers took extra care to protect the sheep from harm. There were many wild beasts such as lions and wolves that would like nothing more than a sheep to eat.

To keep these animals from eating their precious sheep, the villagers trusted a boy to take good care of the flocks. This boy was named Wolfgang.

Each morning the boy gathered the sheep into one flock. Then he would lead them through the fields and pastures until he found the greenest grass. When the sheep were thirsty, Wolfgang led them to babbling brooks of water.

One day, Wolfgang began to daydream. He imagined that a wolf was after his flock, and that he bravely fought it off.

This daydream got him thinking: What would happen if a wolf really *did* come after his sheep? In all his days as the shepherd boy, Wolfgang had never had to deal with a wild animal. He was just a boy, and no match for a hungry, growling, prowling wolf!

Worried about what might happen if a wolf *did* attack the flock, Wolfgang wanted to see if the villagers would come to his aid.

His hand up to his mouth, Wolfgang called out in his most frightened voice, "Help! A wolf! A wolf!"

As Wolfgang had hoped, the people of the village came running to help. The village band dropped its tubas and accordions. The tavern girls dropped their mugs and plates. The farmers dropped their plows and milk buckets. Soon the entire village was in the pasture, ready to save poor Wolfgang and his sheep from a wolf that was not there.

"I heard Wolfgang cry 'Wolf!'" said the tuba player. "I cut short my polka."

"I heard Wolfgang call," said a tavern girl. "I left my customers to come help."

"I heard Wolfgang crying that there was a wolf," said a farmer. "Why, I knocked over a morning's worth of milk as I ran to help!"

As the people of the village came to his rescue, Wolfgang found it funny. He laughed as the tuba player waddled along. He giggled as the tavern girl tripped over her apron. He howled as the farmer's hat flew off his head.

Alas, the people of the village did not find the prank as funny as Wolfgang did.

"There's no wolf?" asked the tubist.

"Wolfgang lied!" said the tavern girl.

"He's in trouble!" said the schoolmarm.

The farmer scolded, "You have lied to us. If a wolf attacks your sheep, you shouldn't expect us to come to your rescue."

Wolfgang held his head in shame. He had done wrong. He would never lie again.

Once the people of the village had left, Wolfgang sat down upon the grassy hill. As Wolfgang was thinking about his lie and the trouble it had caused, you would never believe what crept up behind him... .

That's right—a real-life WOLF!

The beast chased the lambs, hungrily licking its lips. The snarling animal scattered the ewes, snapping its jaws. The growling canine stormed up the hill, glaring at poor Wolfgang with its glowing eyes.

Wolfgang didn't know what to do. So he ran. And he screamed and yelled for help.

"Help! Help!" Wolfgang cried. "A wolf! A wolf! Please save me from this awful wolf!"

Wolfgang dashed into the village. He ran down the streets of Schaffenburg, crying out that a wolf was after his sheep. Just as the farmer had warned, nobody came to help.

"He is lying," said the schoolmarm.

"Fiddlesticks," said the tavern girl. "That Wolfgang is trying to trick us."

The tuba player kept playing his polka, sure that Wolfgang wasn't telling the truth.

As the people of Schaffenburg went about their daily business, that wolf chased off the entire flock of sheep!

That day, Wolfgang learned that nobody believes a liar, even when he tells the truth.

Tom Sawyer

Adapted from the novel by Mark Twain
Illustrated by David Austin Clar

It was a sunny, summer Saturday and all was right with the world. St. Petersburg basked in the warmth of the sun. Birds sang. The laughter of the town's children, playing games of tag and leapfrog, echoed among the trees and red-brick homes.

Yes, all was right with the world — for everyone but Tom Sawyer.

Poor Tom watched his friends frolic and run. He watched the mighty steamboats chug up and down the muddy river. But watch was all Tom could do, for he had a fence to paint.

As he stood painting the fence, Tom heard a voice singing a funny song.

"Buffalo girls, won't you come out tonight, come out tonight, come out tonight?"

The voice was getting closer, and Tom recognized it was his friend Jim!

"Jim!" Tom said, an idea in his head. "I bet you'd like to paint this fence, huh?"

"Oh, Tom," said Jim, "I don't believe I can do that. Your Aunt Polly warned me you would try to get me to do your work."

"This is hardly work at all," said Tom. "It's fun! I'll sit and read that comic book of yours while you paint the fence. Why, I'll even show you my sore toe."

A sore toe isn't something you see every day. Especially a sore toe that was wrapped in a bandage. Jim agreed to help paint the fence for a quick peek—just one, small peek—at Tom's sore toe.

"This sure is a funny comic book," Tom laughed. He watched Jim paint away.

Just then a voice called from the house. "Tom Sawyer," it said, "I told you to paint that fence by yourself!" It was Aunt Polly!

As Aunt Polly came roaring out the front door, Jim scooted down the street, his comic book in his hand. Tom picked up his brush and paint bucket and got back to painting the fence.

Tom began to think of the fun he would be having if it weren't for Aunt Polly and her fence. He could be on some wild adventure, or watching the steamboats chug past.

As Tom thought of the steamboats that cruised the mighty Mississippi, he *heard* a steamboat—and it sounded awfully close.

Ding-dong! Toot-toot!

Tom saw Ben Rogers pretending to be the grand steamboat, the *Big Missouri.*

"Starboard!" Ben yelled, turning his toy wheel. "Men, we're taking on water! Stop her, sir! *Ting-a-ling! Toot-toot!*"

Tom tried to ignore all of the fun Ben was having. But it was hard to do.

"Hi there, Tom," Ben said.

Tom pretended his friend wasn't there.

"You have to work today, huh?" asked Ben, holding a crisp, red apple. "Too bad. I'm going swimming. I bet you'd rather work."

"Work?" Tom asked, a plan in his head. "This isn't work. Painting is loads of fun!"

"It's not every day that you get to paint," said Ben. "Can I try?"

"I can't let you," Tom said. "You see, my Aunt Polly is awful set on how she wants her fence painted. You might mess it all up."

But Ben Rogers wanted to paint that old fence more than anything in the whole world.

"I'll give you my apple," Ben offered.

Ben handed his apple to Tom. And Tom pretended to be sad as he handed the brush to Ben. But deep inside, Tom was happy to get out of the work.

Soon, Tom was surrounded by all of the children of St. Petersburg. They saw how Ben wanted to paint. *They* wanted to paint, too!

Tom sat munching his apple, planning how he would trick the rest of the children.

Once Ben Rogers was done, Tom let Billy Fisher paint—after Billy handed over his new kite. Once Billy was tired, Tom gave Johnny Miller the chance to paint for some bottle caps and a jaw harp.

Soon the happiest boy in St. Petersburg was Tom Sawyer. He now had a jaw harp, a toy cannon, a key, a few pieces of chalk, a new collection of bottle caps, a toy soldier, a tadpole, a kitten, a brilliant brass doorknob, and a dog collar.

Yes, Tom was the happiest boy in town, sitting in the shade while his friends painted.

The North Wind

Adapted from the Norse folktale
Illustrated by Beth Foster Wiggins

In the land of Norway, there once lived a poor widow who had a son named Ivar. Ivar's mother was often sick. One day she said, "I am not feeling well. Could you please get some grain so that we can eat?"

Ivar, a loving son, said that he would. He set off to get a basketful of grain.

As Ivar walked home, the North Wind came along. Blustering and blowing, the North Wind blew away all of Ivar's grain.

Ivar decided he would ask the North Wind to give the grain back.

The journey to the North Wind's house was long. Ivar finally arrived at the door of the North Wind and called out, "Hello!"

The North Wind answered back in his blustery voice, "Hello to you! Thank you for coming to visit me. How can I help you?"

"Will you give me back the grain that you blew out of my basket?" Ivar asked. "My mother and I are so poor and hungry."

"I do not have your grain," said the North Wind. "But I will give you a magic tablecloth. Say, 'Cloth, spread yourself,' and it will serve you all sorts of good food."

Ivar took the tablecloth and left. It was such a long trip that he stopped at an inn.

Inside the inn, Ivar placed the tablecloth on a table and said, "Cloth, spread yourself." The tablecloth did as the North Wind had promised. There on the table was an entire delicious meal laid out: juicy roast beef, ripe vegetables, a tasty cake, and hearty bread.

Ivar was amazed. He ate and ate.

Another person had seen the tablecloth do its magic and was just as amazed. The innkeeper, a bad man, had watched the trick.

Once Ivar was fast asleep, the innkeeper took the magic tablecloth from the boy's sack. He put a regular tablecloth in its place.

The next day, Ivar awoke. Not knowing he'd been tricked, the boy headed home.

When Ivar arrived at home, he told his mother about the magic tablecloth. "We'll have plenty to eat!" he said.

But when the boy put the tablecloth on the table, nothing happened! Not one piece of food appeared. Ivar was disappointed. The tablecloth had worked its magic the day before. Why wasn't it working now?

"The only thing to do is for me to go back to the North Wind's house and tell him what is wrong," Ivar told his mother.

With that, Ivar walked and walked until he again arrived at the North Wind's house, and said, "You've given me this worthless tablecloth. It will not do what you said."

"Why don't you take this magic bank?" the North Wind offered. "If you tell the bank, 'Rain, bank! Make money!' it will make you gold coins."

So Ivar took the magic bank and headed home. Once again, he stopped at the inn for the night. Inside, Ivar took out the bank and said, "Rain, bank! Make money!" The bank began to spit out shiny coins of gold.

But once Ivar was asleep, the innkeeper sneaked into the boy's room and took the magic bank from his sack. The innkeeper replaced the magic bank with a regular one.

Not knowing he'd been tricked, Ivar took his sack and headed home the next day.

Once home, Ivar said, "Rain, bank! Make money!" but nothing happened!

This time, Ivar was very disappointed. The tablecloth hadn't worked, and now the bank didn't work. "The only thing to do is for me to go back to the North Wind's house and tell him what is wrong," Ivar said.

With that, the boy walked and walked, until he arrived at the door of the North Wind. He knocked on the door and said, "This bank will not do what you said."

"All I have left is this magic rope," said the North Wind. "Say, 'Rope, rope, tie on,' and it will tie up whatever you like. Now watch out for that sneaky innkeeper."

Ivar took the magic rope and stopped at the same inn as before. Suspicious, Ivar climbed into bed and pretended to sleep.

As soon as he heard Ivar's snoring, the innkeeper crept into the boy's room, intent on stealing whatever the boy had in his sack. Just as the innkeeper was about to pick up the rope, Ivar shouted, "Rope, rope, tie on!"

Like a snake, the rope wrapped itself around the innkeeper. It tied up his hands and feet. "Help!" the innkeeper cried. "Let me loose!" Ivar only let the innkeeper go once he had his magic tablecloth and bank back. Then Ivar headed home, where he and his mother were never poor or hungry again.

The Bell of Justice

Adapted from the ballad by Henry Wadsworth Longfellow
Illustrated by Jon Goodell

here once was a small and humble town called Atri.

One day King John's procession came through Atri. When King John reached the town square, he said, "By royal order, a bell shall hang here. When anyone is wronged, ring the bell. When this Bell of Justice is rung, the town's judge shall correct whatever wrong has been done." And so a bell hung in the square and the king's orders were obeyed.

For many years, the Bell of Justice rang when wrongs were done. When livestock was stolen, the farmer rang the bell. When a grandmother's fruit pie was swiped, she rang the bell. When a child was bullied, he or she rang the bell. In every case, the judge would bring justice to those who had done wrong.

Yet Atri's love for the Bell of Justice ended. After many years of not being used, the bell rusted, and its rope fell off.

Although Atri had forgotten about the Bell of Justice, the town's judge had not. He called to one man and said, "Please go into the woods and get a vine. We will tie the vine to the bell so that it can be rung again."

Since the rule of King John, other things had changed besides the Bell of Justice. During King John's reign, there had been a gallant knight called the Knight of Atri. Tales of his adventures were still told. Yet knights, just like bells, grow rusty with age.

The Knight of Atri was no different. His hair had grown gray. His sword and shield had rusted. He had sold his horses, hawks, and hounds, his vineyards and his gardens. The old Knight of Atri was content to count the piles of gold coins that he had made from selling everything he owned.

The only thing he kept was the horse who had so often carried him into battle.

But the knight did not take good care of the horse. "Why should I bother with this old beast?" the old knight often asked. "I don't use him anymore, so why should I feed or take good care of him?"

By looking at the old horse, one could tell how poorly the knight cared for him. He was very thin and his eyes were tired and sad. The poor horse looked old and hungry.

One day the horse went to the knight, begging for a bit of grain or hay to eat.

"It's not a holiday, so I don't see why you should expect to be fed," said the knight. With that, the Knight of Atri turned away his once-favorite horse, and faithful companion.

The tired old horse trudged out into the hot summer sun, his belly begging to eat. The horse wandered through pastures, finding no grass to nibble. The horse wandered through fields, finding no corn to eat. The Knight of Atri's horse finally wandered into the town of Atri, hoping to find something to eat there.

But as the horse walked the streets, food was hard to find. The dogs of the town barked at the horse and chased him. The people shut their doors and windows on this hot day, hoping to keep the heat out. The heat persisted, lulling them to sleep.

The horse spotted the square, where a green vine hung from the Bell of Justice.

The horse hurried to the Bell of Justice. While horses do not know about such things as bells, they *do* know that a green vine can fill an empty stomach.

It was with this knowledge that the hungry horse grabbed the vine that was tied to the Bell of Justice. The vine had been tied to the end of the bell's old, tattered rope rather tightly and the horse could not pull it loose. The horse pulled, and the bell rang.

The bell rang so loudly that all of the people awoke from their naps. They opened their doors and windows, wondering what the ruckus was. They came out, wondering why the Bell of Justice was being rung.

The people went to the bell, where they found the hungry horse munching on the vine. At the front of the crowd stood the judge. Knowing that the horse belonged to the Knight of Atri, the judge sent for him. When the old knight arrived, the judge said:

What good, what honor, what repute
Can come from starving this poor brute?
Therefore I decree that as this steed
Served you in youth, you shall take heed
To comfort his old age, and to provide
Shelter, food, and field beside.

From that day forth, the knight took care of his horse, and the town never forgot the good that the Bell of Justice could bring.

Rip Van Winkle

Adapted from the story
by Washington Irving
Illustrated by John Lund

As you journey up the long Hudson River, you will be struck by the beauty of the Catskill Mountains. Rising up to the west, these mountains look different with each change in weather or time of day. When the day is cloudless, the Catskill Mountains hold a misty blanket around themselves, glowing with the rays of the setting sun.

There, magic can take place. A magical thing once happened to a man named Rip Van Winkle, a man well-known in his village at the foot of the Catskill Mountains.

Rip Van Winkle lived in a house he had built with his own two hands. He had a wife who took care of their many children. The children were rosy-cheeked and happy, and they all loved their father. Rip would gather his children around him and play games with them. Late at night around the fireplace, Rip would tell the children stories of mystery and magic. Rip Van Winkle was a good father and a good man who enjoyed his life.

Rip's favorite thing to do was hike among the beautiful Catskill Mountains with his beloved dog, Wolf. It was on such an evening hike that Rip's famous troubles would occur.

That evening, as Rip and his dog climbed, a strange voice called Rip's name.

"Rip Van Winkle!" the voice cried. "Rip Van Winkle!" It seemed to be getting closer.

Rip looked around, but saw only an old crow perched in a tree. Figuring that his imagination was playing tricks on him, Rip began to hike again. But again the voice called his name, "Rip Van Winkle!"

Rip turned around and spotted a small figure walking toward him. As the stranger came closer, Rip was surprised. The stranger was a short and stout man with a long, bushy beard. The man carried a barrel. He asked Rip for help, and Rip agreed.

Rip and the man carried the barrel. They went higher into the mountains.

Finally, the two came to a clearing. Here Rip spotted a group of small men much like his new friend. These men were bowling on the grass. The little men all had long, flowing beards and the same funny hats and clothes.

The men opened the barrel, which was full of a dark liquid. Pouring the liquid into mugs, the men offered one to Rip. He found the drink to be so good that he drank mug after mug. The strange little men watched Rip drink. Soon, Rip's head nodded, his eyes closed, and he was sound asleep.

When Rip awoke, he found himself not in the clearing, but lying at the foot of the mountains where he met the strange man.

"I must have slept here all night long! What will I tell my wife?" Rip thought.

Rip called out to his dog so that they could head home. "Come here, boy!" But Wolf would not come.

Rip headed into the village. There, people began to point at Rip. Wondering why they did this, Rip stroked his chin. There he felt a long beard. His clothes were in tatters. The other people were dressed in clothes that seemed strange to Rip. Even the buildings were different, with new paint and signs.

Rip left the village. He walked until he got to where his warm, sturdy home stood. As he came to the house, he expected to hear his wife's voice, scolding him for not coming home the night before. He expected to hear his children playing and his dog barking.

But Rip Van Winkle did not hear his wife or children. And he did not see the house he had left behind the night before. Instead, the house had fallen apart with age.

Then Rip heard a dog bark. This dog looked a lot like Rip's old dog, but it didn't come when he called it. Rip knew it couldn't be his faithful Wolf.

Rip wandered back into the village. The people gathered around Rip, still pointing at him. They asked who he was, worried that he was crazy or even dangerous.

A man with a hat hushed the crowd. "Leave this fellow alone," he said. He asked Rip who he was, and why he was there.

"I've lived here my whole life," Rip said.

"Name the people here," the man said.

"Nicholas Vedder, Brom Dutcher … ," Rip told the people of the crowd.

"Nicholas Vedder has been gone for years," said the man. "And Brom Dutcher went off to war."

Rip's heart sank. The changes in his home and friends made him sad. Rip saw a familiar woman. "What is your father's name?" he asked.

"My father's name was Rip Van Winkle. He left us twenty years ago."

"*I* am Rip Van Winkle," Rip said.

The crowd looked closer at Rip. This man *did* look like Rip Van Winkle. He was telling the truth! The man whom they had not seen in twenty years had come home!

That night all the people of the town welcomed Rip home, after twenty long years sleeping in the Catskill Mountains. The story of Rip Van Winkle became a legend.

Prince Carrots

Adapted from the fairy tale
Illustrated by Kathy Mitchell

Long ago, there were many kings and queens. Their children were princes and princesses. One of these princes was Prince Carrots. He was hard to look at. His head was too wide. His mouth was too big. And he had orange hair. That is why he was called Prince Carrots.

This upset his mother, the queen.

"You must not worry," said Mercury the Magician. "The prince will be intelligent. I can give him a special gift. He can give his intelligence to the person he loves the most."

Every year, the prince's face grew wider. His nose grew longer. His mouth grew bigger. His hair became a brighter orange. But he was very intelligent. The king asked him questions, such as about the Trojan War.

"Helen was kidnapped from Greece by a Trojan named Paris," Prince Carrots said. "Greek soldiers hid in a wooden horse that was taken to the gates of Troy. They spilled out of the horse and attacked Troy to rescue Helen because she was very beautiful."

The queen asked where pearls are from.

"From an oyster," Prince Carrots said. "When sand gets in its shell, it makes a pearl. See, even sand can become beautiful."

Prince Carrots also made people laugh. "Carrots are good for eyes," he said. "Except Prince Carrots," was the reply.

Everyone tried not to laugh. It wasn't nice to make fun of the prince, who replied, "Have you ever seen a rabbit with glasses?"

Everyone laughed. The prince smiled.

One day, a princess from a nearby kingdom noticed the prince's nice smile.

Prince Carrots was surprised that this princess would look at him, because she was the most beautiful girl he had ever seen.

Prince Carrots could not look away from this beautiful princess. He went to her and introduced himself.

"I am Prince Carrots," he said.

"I am Princess Pia," she said.

"I am honored to meet you," he said.

"I am honored to meet you," she said.

He was shocked. No princess was ever honored to meet him. "I have been told that you are smart," she said. Still, she did not smile. The princess was sad.

"Why are you unhappy?" he asked her.

"I wish I were smart," Pia said.

"But you are very beautiful," he said.

"Yes," she said. "I have heard that a thousand times." Princess Pia told Prince Carrots that she only remembered things if she heard them a thousand times.

"My mother has a magician friend," the princess said. "When I was young, she told him she was worried that I was beautiful but not very smart."

"You *are* beautiful," the prince said.

"But not smart," the princess said. "My mother wanted him to make me intelligent. He told her I would be loved for my beauty."

The prince listened intently.

"My mother was still worried," she said. "The magician told her I would be able to give my beauty to someone. I could give it to the person I loved the most."

The prince nodded again. Princess Pia and he were a lot alike.

The two spent the day together.

Prince Carrots heard the story about Mercury the Magician many times. The princess could not remember that she had already told him.

But Prince Carrots did not mind.

The prince was a good listener. But he was hard to look at. When Pia looked away, he did not seem to mind. She liked that.

The prince loved the way he felt around her. She did not ask questions. She did not expect him to tell jokes. He did not feel ugly when he was with her.

"You are dear to me," the prince said.

"You are dear to me," the princess said.

When they parted, Prince Carrots missed Princess Pia. He wanted to see her, and she wanted to see the prince.

"She is lovely even when her hair is tangled," the prince thought.

"He is smart to repeat things so I will remember," the princess thought.

"Will you marry me?" the prince asked.

"Yes!" the princess answered.

Everyone was shocked when they heard the news.

No one could believe it but Mercury the Magician. He knew that there is one thing even better than being smart or beautiful— being loved just the way you are.

The Little Dutch Boy

Adapted from the story by Mary Mapes Dodge
Illustrated by Linda Dockey Graves

In the Dutch city of Haarlem, there lived a kind little boy named Hans. His father tended the dikes, or stone walls, that kept the seawater from rushing into Haarlem and washing it away.

One day, Hans's father left for a trip. Since he spent his days watching his father care for the dikes, Hans had nothing to do. "Take this basket of bread to Mr. Jansen," Hans's mother said. Hans happily agreed.

As Hans walked to Mr. Jansen's house, he passed the dikes. The spring rains had filled the dikes to the top. His father gone, Hans wondered who would tend the dikes.

Hans pressed on as it rained. He hunched his shoulders and pulled his coat tight, trying to keep the chill out.

Hans pulled his hat down around his ears. The boy shivered as the cold, hard rain pelted him, but he kept on walking.

The rains this spring were heavier than usual, pouring down hard day and night. While the wind turned the windmills, and the rain watered the tulips, the swollen dikes kept filling, worrying Hans as he passed.

Hans reached Mr. Jansen's house with the basket of bread. Mr. Jansen was an old man who had no one to care for him. He was one of many sick or poor people whom Hans's mother cared for.

Mr. Jansen was overjoyed that Hans had come. "Sit down," the old man said. "The bread you have brought me smells delicious!"

Hans pulled the loaf from the basket and they shared the fresh bread.

Mr. Jansen enjoyed telling the boy his stories about how things were long ago, and about the history of Haarlem and Holland. And Hans loved to listen.

The old man and the boy talked and
talked. They laughed and laughed. They ate
all of the bread. It was soon very late. Hans
didn't realize where the time had gone.

Hans said good night and began the long
walk home. He was sad to see that the rain
had not let up. "This will make for a cold
and wet walk," Hans thought to himself as
the rain pattered onto his coat and hat.

The rain began to fall harder. Hans
walked faster, the raindrops chilling him.
He wanted a warm dinner and his cozy bed.

The rain fell harder and harder. Hans
knew that his mother must be worried. Cold
and tired, he began to run toward home.

Hans ran and ran, past the tulips and the windmills. His wooden shoes clicked on the brick road and kept his feet warm and dry from the sloshy mud and puddles.

Hans was running when he passed one of the dikes. Something was not right. Hans crept closer to the dike. In a crack between the stone blocks was a small hole. From the hole seeped a small trickle of water.

While the water looked harmless, Hans knew that the water behind the wall would push at the tiny hole until it became bigger. Soon the water would rush through, washing away the town. Hans stuck his fist into the hole, plugging it up.

Hans stood at the leaking dike with his fist stuck in the hole, his hand the only thing keeping the water from washing away the town of Haarlem.

Hans's mother did not know the trouble that her son had discovered. She did not know that he was stuck in the storm, soaked to the bone from the rain.

"Hans!" she called from the door of their house. "Hans, where are you?"

If only her husband were home, she thought. He would bravely venture into the storm and find their beloved son. Little did she know that Hans was showing bravery of his own.

The rain pelted Hans, and the wind swirled. But the boy kept his hand in the hole. He knew that to save his town, he could not let the water through the dike.

"Help!" Hans called out.

Suddenly, there was old Mr. Jansen.

"I heard you calling for help," the old man said. Mr. Jansen brought with him some of the townsfolk to repair the hole in the dike.

"Let's get you home," said Mr. Jansen. The old man walked Hans back home and told Hans's mother about his bravery. Soon everyone in town heard about Hans, the brave little Dutch boy, who saved the town.

Rikki-Tikki-Tavi

Adapted from the story
by Rudyard Kipling
Illustrated by Richard Bernal

Rikki-tikki-tavi was a mongoose, a small animal that has the fur and tail of a cat with the head of a weasel.

One day, a flood came through a hole that Rikki-tikki-tavi lived in. The rush of water carried the mongoose far away from his home. He was sick, cold, and wet.

Luckily, a small boy named Teddy found the mongoose. Teddy picked up Rikki-tikki-tavi and brought him inside his family's bungalow where it was warm and dry. The boy saved the mongoose's life that day.

Teddy showed the wet little mongoose to
his parents.

Teddy's mother brought a towel into the
kitchen and wrapped Rikki-tikki-tavi in it.
Warm and dry, the little mongoose opened
his eyes and let out a wet mongoose sneeze.

Rikki-tikki-tavi began to look around, as
members of the mongoose family are curious.
He sniffed at Teddy and gave the boy a lick.

"I think he's so friendly because you
saved his life," said Teddy's father.

"Can we keep him?" Teddy asked.

"What if he bites?" asked Teddy's mother.

"Rubbish!" said Teddy's father.

Teddy's father knew that snakes and mongooses are enemies. If a snake ever got into the house, Rikki-tikki-tavi could help protect the family.

Mongooses are one of the few animals that can win a fight with a snake. And it wouldn't be long before Rikki-tikki-tavi would meet one.

One day Rikki-tikki-tavi was with his bird friend, Darzee, when they heard a rustle in the bushes.

"Oh, no," said Darzee. "It's Nag!"

"Who is Nag?" Rikki-tikki-tavi asked.

"I am Nag," said a large cobra that came slithering out from the brush.

"Be afraid!" hissed Nag.

But Rikki-tikki-tavi was not afraid. He knew that the life of a mongoose was spent catching snakes like Nag.

That night, Rikki-tikki-tavi was in the bungalow when he heard a noise. He spotted Nag and his cobra wife, Nagaina.

"We must empty this house of people," Nagaina said.

"Yes," agreed Nag. "If we get rid of the people, then the mongoose cannot stay."

The two snakes slithered up the stairs toward one of the bedrooms. Rikki-tikki-tavi followed them.

At the top of the stairs, Rikki-tikki-tavi saw his chance. Jumping, he lunged at Nag.

"No!" screamed Nag. The cobra thrashed, trying to shake the little mongoose off, but it was no use. Rikki-tikki-tavi held on tight. If he had let go, Nag could have bitten him and gone after Teddy.

The snake and the mongoose thrashed and crashed all around the hallway.

Suddenly there was a loud *THUD!* Rikki-tikki-tavi looked up to see Teddy's father holding a broomstick. Teddy's dad had hit Nag with the broomstick. With the man's help, Rikki-tikki-tavi had stopped the evil and vicious cobra.

"Bad Nag is gone, gone, gone," Rikki-tikki-tavi heard someone sing. It was Darzee.

"Where's Nagaina?" the mongoose asked.

"Guarding her nest," Darzee said. "She has a bunch of eggs that will hatch soon."

"Where is this nest?" Rikki-tikki-tavi asked the bird. Darzee told him.

"You must pretend that your wing is hurt, in order to lure Nagaina away from her nest. Then I will steal away all of her eggs. Once I take care of Nagaina, we will be safe," Rikki-tikki-tavi said to the bird.

Darzee distracted Nagaina, and Rikki-tikki-tavi got rid of the eggs. But then Nagaina saw what Rikki-tikki-tavi was doing.

Quickly, Nagaina slithered over and snatched up her last egg. The cobra tried to escape, but Rikki-tikki-tavi knew that Nagaina would be back.

The mongoose chased the cobra deep into the wetlands. Rikki-tikki-tavi's courage scared the cobra so much that Nagaina was never seen again.

Rikki-tikki-tavi celebrated with Darzee and their other animal friends. The cobras were gone and everyone was safe!

As for Teddy's family, they never saw a cobra ever again! Rikki-tikki-tavi had saved his family, and they lived happily ever after.

Stone Soup

Adapted from the traditional folktale
Illustrated by Barbara Lanza

ack Grand walked along with a feather in his hat, and a smile on his face.

Jack Grand was a rat-a-tat man. He could do all sorts of things. He could dance. He could walk on his hands. He could yodel. He could hum. He could play the drum. He could whittle. He even knew riddles.

Jack had a good life. But often, he was hungry. He had not eaten in many days. He walked until he saw a village. "Where there's a village, there are people. Where there are people, there is food," Jack thought.

Jack came upon a house. A name was
painted on the gate: TUBBS. An old man
opened the door. Jack bowed and said,
"I'm Jack Grand, the rat-a-tat man."

"I have no money," said Mr. Tubbs.

"I understand," Jack said. "I'm hungry."

"I only have salt and pepper," said Mr.
Tubbs. "Ask Miss Grubbs next door."

A thin lady answered at the next house.

"Hello, Miss Grubbs," Jack said. "I'm Jack
Grand, the rat-a-tat man."

"I have no money," said Miss Grubbs.

"The truth is," Jack said, "I'm hungry."

"I have only a head of garlic," said Miss
Grubbs. "Ask Mrs. Chubbs next door."

A plump woman answered at the next house. Jack said, "Hello, Mrs. Chubbs, I'm Jack Grand, the rat-a-tat man."

"I have no money," said Mrs. Chubbs.

"I'm so hungry," Jack said.

"I have only a few potatoes," said Mrs. Chubbs. "Ask someone else."

Jack knocked on every door. One woman had only cabbage. Her neighbor had only carrots. One family had only a bit of bacon. Another family had only a handful of beans.

Jack walked along for a while. He saw a stone. The stone gave Jack an idea.

He picked it up and examined it. "Perfect," Jack said to himself.

Jack ran back to town. He knocked on the first door. Mr. Tubbs answered.

"You have no food to share," Jack said. "But do you have a big pot I could borrow?"

"A big pot?" asked Mr. Tubbs. "What have you got there, son?"

"It's a soup stone," Jack said.

"A soup stone?" asked Mr. Tubbs.

"To make soup," Jack said.

Mr. Tubbs came out with a big pot.

Jack carried the big pot to the village square. He filled it with water. He built a fire underneath it and dropped the stone in.

The pot bubbled. Jack dipped his spoon into the water. He tasted it. "Perfect," he said.

"It would be better with a little salt and pepper," said Jack, "Not much. Just a little."

"I have salt and pepper," said Mr. Tubbs. He ran to his cottage and returned with a salt shaker and a pepper mill.

Jack sprinkled the salt into the pot. He ground the pepper into the pot. It bubbled. Jack dipped his spoon into the pot and tasted the soup. "Perfect," he said.

Miss Grubbs came out of her cottage. She had been watching Jack. She came over and peeked into the pot.

"It's stone soup," said Mr. Tubbs.

"Is it good?" asked Miss Grubbs.

"It would be better with a little garlic," said Jack, "Not much. Just a little."

"I have garlic," said Miss Grubbs. She ran to her cottage and returned with garlic.

Jack chopped the head of garlic. He sprinkled the garlic into the pot and stirred.

The pot bubbled. Jack dipped his spoon into the pot. He tasted the stone soup. "Perfect," he said.

Mrs. Chubbs came out of her cottage. She had been watching Jack, too. She came over and peeked into the pot, curious as to what it was.

"It's stone soup," said Miss Grubbs.

"Is it any good?" asked Mrs. Chubbs.

Just as Mr. Tubbs and Miss Grubbs had done, Mrs. Chubbs brought the only food she had, and added it to the pot.

Soon, the entire village had gathered. They wanted to know what was in the pot.

A woman ran to get cabbage. A man ran to get carrots. Other villagers ran to get beans and bacon. Jack threw it all into the pot.

Jack spooned soup for everyone. He ate until he was full. The villagers ate until they were full. They ate until the pot was empty.

Empty, that is, except for the stone.

"Use it for your next pot of stone soup," Jack said to the villagers as he headed to another village to meet more new friends.

The
End

Good night!

this book

belongs to

Charles Allard